A NOTE ABOUT THE STORY

The classic tale of Pinocchio, about a puppet boy whose nose grows longer whenever he lies, is a story Tony Johnston loved as a child. So it's no wonder that a Japanese folktale about a magic fan that makes noses grow and shrink would appeal to Tony for a retelling. "The childlike humor and mischief in this story drew me to it at once," she says. "What fun it would be to make your nose shrink and grow as you wanted it to! And if you were feeling especially naughty, it would be even *more* fun to make someone else's nose grow long!"

Tony has added her own scenes and characters, embellishing the skeleton of the tale about the *tengu* goblin children and the mischievous badger. "Over the centuries," she says, "a principal figure in Japanese folklore has been the *tengu*. This is a kind of demon or goblin who usually carries a fan, has a large red nose and represents pride or arrogance. Tengu are 'still seen and talked about' in the villages of Japan."

When I read the manuscript with the task of illustrating it in mind, I saw the story as closer to the feeling of Gilbert and Sullivan's *Mikado* than to the more serious world of Kabuki drama. And although I researched Japanese costumes and settings, especially of the Edo woodcut era, I too took liberties to do my part in adding to the zaniness; especially with the *tengu* children, giving them more charm and mischief, rather than pride.

—*Tomie dePaola, Creative Director,*
WHITEBIRD BOOKS

THE BADGER
AND THE
MAGIC FAN

A Japanese Folktale adapted by
Tony Johnston
illustrated by Tomie dePaola

A WHITEBIRD BOOK
G. P. Putnam's Sons
New York

For Donna and Don McClelland
—TJ

For Ruth Gottstein, who loves Japan
—TdeP

Text copyright © 1990 by Tony Johnston
Illustrations copyright © 1990 by Tomie dePaola
All rights reserved. This book, or parts thereof,
may not be reproduced in any form without
permission in writing from the publisher.
G.P. Putnam's Sons, a division of
The Putnam & Grosset Group,
200 Madison Avenue, New York, NY 10016.
Published simultaneously in Canada.
Printed in Hong Kong by South China Printing Co. (1988) Ltd.
Type design by Gunta Alexander
Library of Congress Cataloging-in-Publication Data
Johnston, Tony. The badger and the magic fan. "A Whitebird book."
Summary: Stealing the young goblins' magic fan, a badger makes
a fortune after using the fan to make a rich girl's nose grow.
[1. Folklore—Japan] I. dePaola, Tomie, ill. II. Title.
PZ8.1.J643Bad 1990 398.21'0952 [E] 89-4027
ISBN 0-399-21945-5
1 3 5 7 9 10 8 6 4 2
First impression

Tengu are the goblins of Japan. And you can spot them in a minute because they have very long noses.

Once three little tengu children were playing with a magic fan. They laughed and giggled all the time for when they fanned with one side of the fan, their noses grew longer still. When they fanned with the other side, they shrank right back again. Back and forth. Long and short. What a fine time they were having!

A badger happened along and watched the children play.
"Ho-ho!" he thought. *"How I would love such a fan!"*
Then he thought of a way to get it.

Now the badgers of Japan can turn themselves into any-
thing they want to be. So he turned himself into a little
girl. Then he took a plate of bean-jam buns and skipped
straight up to the tengu children.

"Hello, little tengu children," said the badger in disguise.
"You may have these bean-jam buns if I can play with you."
The tengu children loved bean-jam buns.

But there were four bean-jam buns and only three little
tengu children. So, of course, they began to argue over the
extra bun.

The tricky badger said, "Let's do this. Close your eyes tightly and hold your breath. Whoever keeps his eyes closed and holds his breath the longest gets the extra bean-jam bun."

What a good idea!

The tengu children decided to do just that. For they loved bean-jam buns.

They took deep breaths. They shut their eyes tight. And when they did—that wicked badger grabbed the magic fan and ran away laughing!

Then he changed himself back into a badger and headed
toward the city, laughing all the time.

On the way he came to a temple. Inside sat a beautiful girl
dressed in fine clothes. Her father was as rich as rich can be.

"Ho-ho!" thought the badger. *"Now I will have some fun!"*

He sneaked up behind the girl. *Tiptoe, tiptoe, tiptoe.* He fanned her nose with the magic fan. And—bzzzzzzzzzt!— it grew long, long, long, LONG!

What a fright!

The poor girl hid from sight and cried all the tears out of herself.

Her father pounded his fists and yelled all the yells out of himself.

But this did not help at all.

So her father called all the doctors of Japan together.
They could cure fevers and bunions and warts. Surely
they could shrink a nose.

The doctors had many ideas.
"Feed her thistledown," said one doctor.
"No, sea urchins," said another.
"No, no, no," said a third. "Stuff her with cabbage.
Cabbage is the cure."

The girl ate thistledown (which was tickly). She ate sea urchins (which were prickly). She stuffed herself with cabbage.

But her nose stayed long, long, LONG.

"Fools!" screeched her angry father. "I will cure *you* with cabbages!"

He threw cabbages at the doctors. And they all ran away.

The father sent for a witch, who lived nearby. She could cast spells and turn fish to gold. Surely she could shrink a nose.

"Simply sprinkle pepper on the nose," the witch said. "Then she will sneeze it off."

"Hurry!" cried her frantic father. "Sprinkle away!"

The witch sprinkled pepper on the girl's nose. Lots and lots of pepper.

The girl sneezed. Lots and lots of sneezes. But the nose stayed put.

Her father was so vastly vexed, he sprinkled pepper all over the witch. And she ran away sneezing.

Then the father called all the thinkers of Japan.

"Tie the nose in a knot," suggested one thinker. "Then it will be short."

"Tie it in a bow," said another. "Bows are prettier than knots."

"I'll tie *you* in knots for such silly thoughts!" shouted the girl's father. And he chased them all away.

In despair he cried, "I will give my daughter and half my riches to anyone who can make her nose short again."

"*Ho-ho!*" thought the badger. "*Here is my chance.*"

He hurried straight to the girl's father.

"I shrink noses," he said.

With that, he took out the magic fan and fanned her nose. And—bzzzzzzzzt!—it was short again!

The girl's father was so delighted, he prepared the wedding feast at once.

The badger was so delighted to get a fine (and rich) wife, he ate and ate and ATE at the feast. Then he got very sleepy.

So he lay down, dozed off, and began to snore loudly—
SNNNZZZZZZ.

Now all this time, the tengu children had been searching for that wicked badger to get back their magic fan. They looked in every house, every temple, every palace of Japan.

And with great good luck, at the very moment the badger began to snore, the little tengu children peeked into the rich man's house and saw the badger sleeping there!

So—*tiptoe, tiptoe, tiptoe*—they crept up on silent little tengu feet, took their magic fan, and began fanning his nose with it.

Ho-ho! Did it grow!

The tengu children just smiled and kept fanning. The badger kept snoring. His nose kept growing.

Soon it grew right through the ceiling. It grew up and up
till it poked right through the clouds!

Now, just then, far above the clouds, some heavenly workers were building a bridge across the sky.

"Look!" they shouted when they saw the badger's nose poke through the clouds. "That pole is the perfect size for our bridge! Let's hoist it up!"

So they tugged on the badger's nose. And, my, didn't *that* wake him up?

Soon it grew right through the ceiling. It grew up and up
till it poked right through the clouds!

Now, just then, far above the clouds, some heavenly workers were building a bridge across the sky.

"Look!" they shouted when they saw the badger's nose poke through the clouds. "That pole is the perfect size for our bridge! Let's hoist it up!"

So they tugged on the badger's nose. And, my, didn't *that* wake him up?

"*Ouch-ouch-ouch-help-help-help!*" screamed the badger.

He would have fanned his nose to shrink it again, but the tengu children had kept their magic fan.

"Heave-ho! Up we go!" the heavenly workers chanted.

The badger yelled, "*Yi-yi-yi!*"

And no one ever saw him again. For they pulled that badger right into the sky.

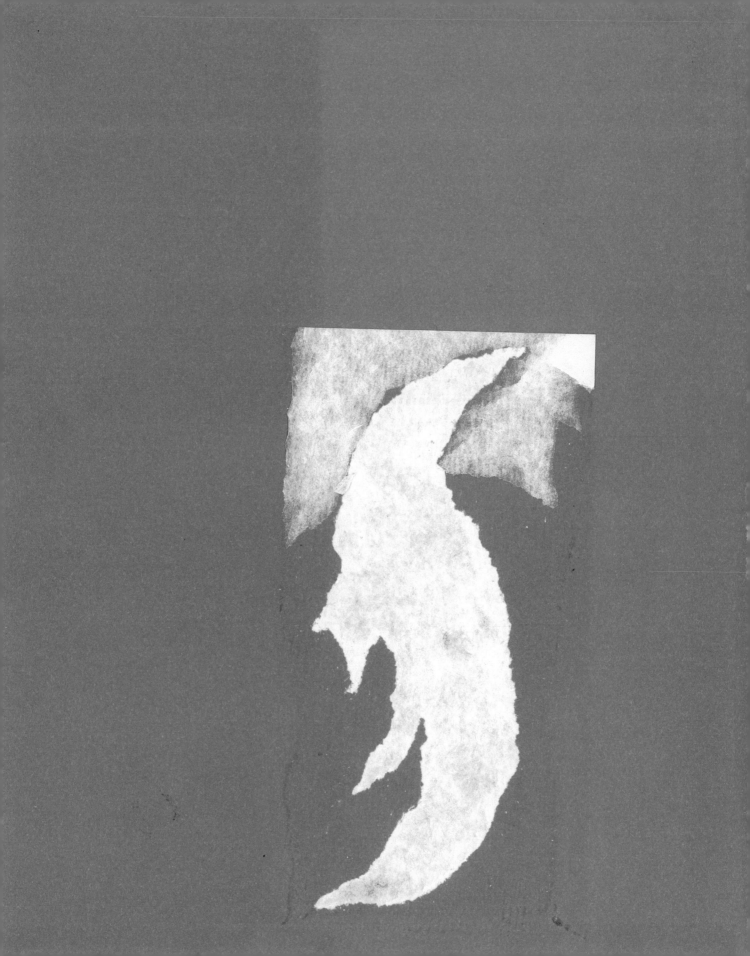